SEARCHING *for...*

The *You* We Adore

To adopted children around the world.
You are loved and adored!
V.W.   R.C.

Published by

SWAN RIVER PUBLISHING, LLC

**www.TheYouWeAdore.com**

Text © 2011 by Valerie Westfall
Illustrations © 2011 by Richard Cowdrey
Edited by Susan K. Elliott
Art Direction by A.D. Creative Group

Printed in Korea, August 2011, 082011-A
Distributed by Swan River Publishing, L.L.C.,
5960 W. Parker Rd. Suite 278 - 324 Plano, TX 75093.
For information: info@SwanRiverPublishing.com

Library of Congress Control Number: 2011908779

Cataloging data available

ISBN: 978-0-9833799-0-4

First Edition 2011

# SEARCHING *for...*
# The *You* We Adore

Written by

## VALERIE WESTFALL

Illustrated by

## RICHARD COWDREY

SWAN RIVER PUBLISHING, LLC

Texas

Our love searched the whole world
for the you we adore.

We longed to open our hearts
to the one we were waiting for.

We dreamt of your smile,
your eyes and your nose.
We couldn't wait to hold you
and tickle your toes.

Our love soared through the clouds
to heaven above.
No distance was too far
to find the one we love.

We sent our love everywhere,
traveling long and far.
It searched for you by the light
of every twinkling star.

We sent our love to Asia
whistling through the leaves,
to see if you were climbing
with the pandas in the trees.

$O$ur love sailed to the islands on a warm, gentle breeze.
It searched for you swimming with the fish in the seas.

We sent our love to Africa,
floating down the Nile,
to see if you were splashing
with the elephants a while.

To faraway places
our love soared and flew.
In the rain forest it talked
to the birds about you.

We sent our love down under, still searching for you.
It peeked in the pouch of every kangaroo.

Our love danced in the sky
    with the northern lights,
looking for you snuggling
    with the cubs, sleeping tight.

Through cities and streets
our dreams held you dear,
hoping one day our loving arms
would hold you near.

We sang you a lullaby softly in the air,
guiding you home safely into our care.

After searching the world
for the you we adore,
you opened our hearts.
You're the one we waited for.

*O*ur love finally found
the one and only you.
Ours for evermore:
**A DREAM COME TRUE.**